To Riley

Copyright © 2020 Erica L. Clymer
Conshohocken, PA USA

For more information visit www.ericalclymer.com

Special thanks to my husband, Anthony.

ISBN: 978-1-7346063-4-8
Library of Congress Control Number: 2020915767

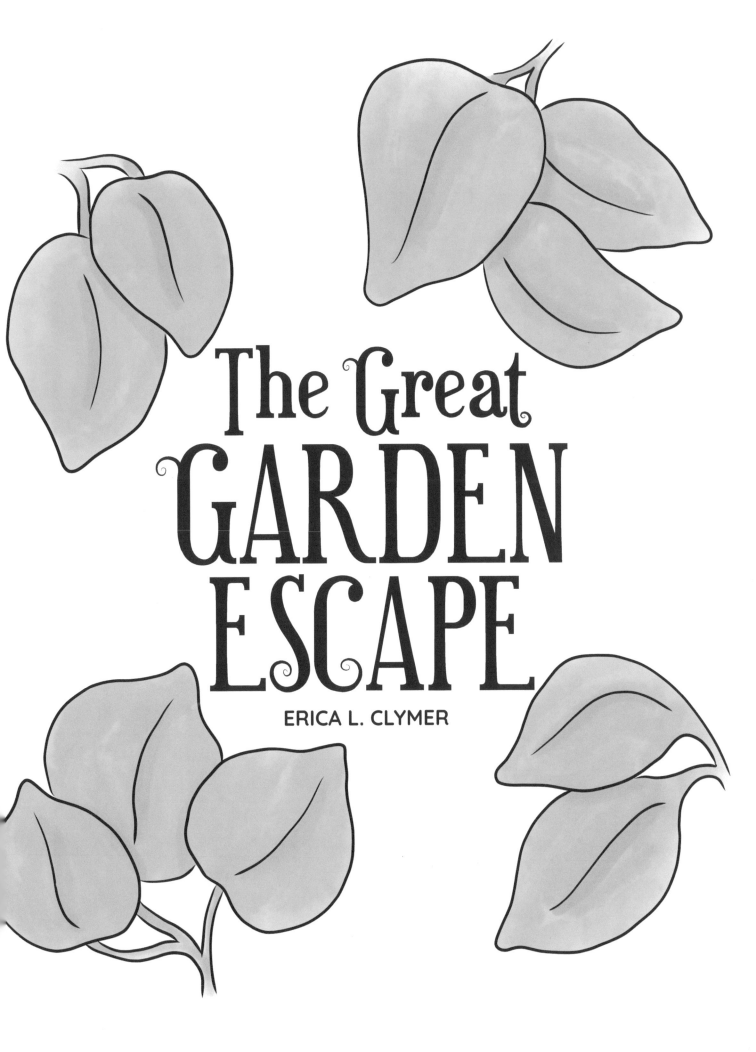

The Great
GARDEN
ESCAPE

ERICA L. CLYMER

The sun beams down in Fruit Garden on this splendid day.
Sally Strawberry and Billy Blueberry are ready to play!

The best friends run through sprinklers on Raspberry Ridge.

They climb Lime Hill and hop over Blackberry Bridge.

Sally and Billy soon reach Mango Mountainside.
The pair race to ride on the Watermelon Slide.

Down they go, zooming faster and faster.
Sally starts to worry, "This might be a disaster!"

At the bottom, Billy yells, "I CAN'T STOPPPPP!"
The two berries fly over Cherry Cliff Drop.

They land on a pile of dirt down below,
in a place where all the vegetables grow.

"That was quite the fall," they suddenly hear.
Sally and Billy see a squash standing near.

"How do we get home to Fruit Garden?" asks Sally.
The squash replies, "Through a secret gate in the Valley."

"There are ten clues that will show you the way.
Find and solve them by the end of today.

The Garden gate locks at sunset, you see.
Hurry! Clue one swings over there, in that tree."

They thank the squash and to the tree, they run.
Sally and Billy read clue number one.

We look like little trees,
but instead of leaves,
our florets
blow in the breeze.

The best friends skip past Radish Region's lot
to investigate the broccoli growing spot.

They search throughout Broccoli Boondocks
and find clue two beneath a pile of rocks.

Sally and Billy zip by the Turnip Town scenery,
on a mission to inspect Carrot County's greenery.

They hop a carrot plant only to see
a lil' ant carrying clue number three.

Through the spears of Asparagus Terrain they go
to arrive on the grounds of Potato Plateau.

Sally and Billy see clue four and squirm.
It's surrounded by a giant, brown worm!

In Brussels Sprout Backwoods, they cautiously tread
until spotting Lettuce Neighborhood just up ahead.

While strolling down Romaine Lane to Iceberg Pike,
Sally and Billy see clue five riding a bright, red bike.

They brush by giant leaves in Cauliflower Grove
to play detectives in the land of Celery Cove.

Just beyond a fallen stalk,
clue six sits perched upon a rock.

A cozy little pod
is where we reside.
We're called Snap, Snow
or even Black-Eyed.

CELERY COVE

The pair steps through Cucumber Plains with ease
on their way to the teeny Park of Peas.

A mushroom shouts, "Where are you going at such a fast pace?"
Sally calls out, "To find our next clue inside Pepper Place."

The ears of corn look quite mystified
as two berries scurry through their Countryside.

In Green Bean Jungle, swinging vine to vine,
Sally and Billy capture clue number nine.

I will not be mistaken
for a Yam.
No, sir. No, Ma'am.
I am NOT a Yam!

GREEN BEAN
JUNGLE

When the two friends appear, the eggplants are aghast!
Never have they ever seen berries move so fast!

Down Sweet Potato Slope they roll
to find clue ten stuck in a hole.

Hold your nose
if you get near.
Our strong smell
makes eyes tear.

"Woo-Hoo! We've solved all the clues!" exclaims Sally.
The best friends high-five and head for the Valley.

Sally and Billy climb Beet Summit's rubble.

Onion Valley looks like nothing but trouble!

They slowly descend into the Valley
and spot the gate down a dreary, dark alley.

The sun has almost set and the gate is about to close.
The pair runs as fast as they can while holding their nose...

Sally and Billy *just* make it through
and collapse to the ground with a...

PHEW!

"I'm happy to be back home," says Billy with a sigh.
The best friends lay in Fruit Garden staring up at the sky.

CPSIA information can be obtained
at www.ICGtesting.com
Printed in the USA
LVHW072304160822
726147LV00007B/37